D0810389

Stories of
Santa

Russell Punter

Illustrated by Philip Webb

Reading Consultant: Alison Kelly
Roehampton University

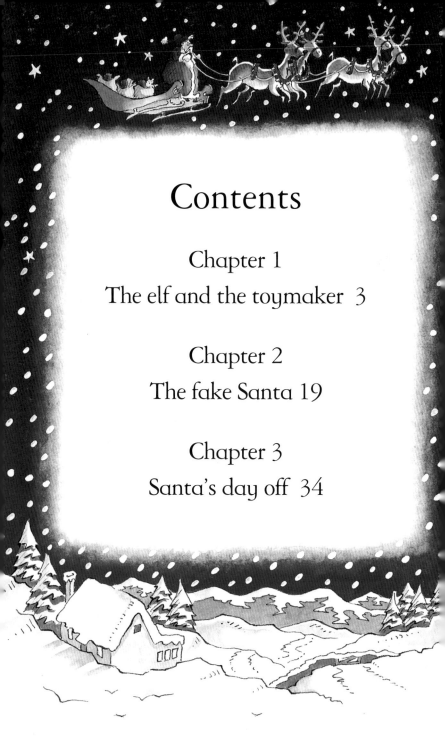

Contents

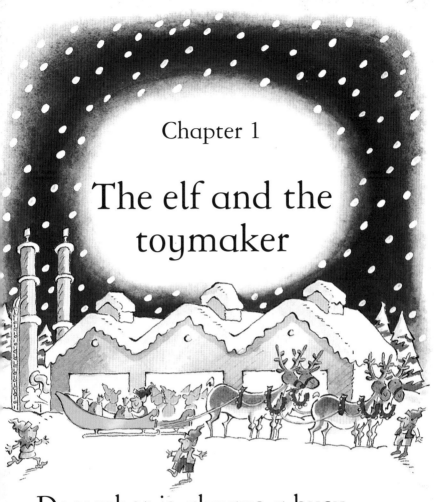

Chapter 1

The elf and the toymaker

December is always a busy time of year at the North Pole. This is the home of Santa's toy factory.

One year, it was especially busy. Santa was touring the factory, making sure things were going to plan.

As usual, his team of tiny elves was hard at work. Each elf had a different job.

Dennis opened the letters sent by boys and girls.

Babs checked whether they'd been good or bad.

Marco read what the good children wanted for Christmas.

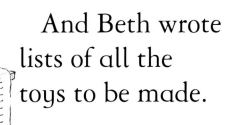

And Beth wrote lists of all the toys to be made.

Paddy and Pip were busy operating the toymaker. Paddy read out the name of a toy.

Pip typed it into a computer.

Alfie was sweeping the store room. He had the most boring job in the factory. It was so boring, he often... fell... aslee...

Zzzzzzzzzzz!

"Wake up, Alfie!" boomed Santa. "It's time to go home."

"Already?" yawned Alfie.

"You're always asleep on the job," complained Santa.

"Go home," he ordered, "and don't come back tomorrow unless you're wide awake."

It's not fair.

Alfie trudged through the deserted factory. "If I was in charge of the toymaker, I'd never be bored," he sighed.

9

Alfie had often wanted a closer look at the magical machine. Now was his chance.

Climbing on top, he peeked down the main tube.

But he lost his balance...

and fell in!

Hours later, Alfie awoke surrounded by cogs and wires.

"I must have knocked myself out," he thought.

Suddenly, Alfie felt the walls shake. Paddy and Pip had started up the machine.

"Oh no!" yelled Alfie. "I'll be squished to pieces."

11

Alfie scrambled around in panic, trying to get out. But the more he wriggled, the more he got tangled in the wiring.

Alfie's wriggling had an odd effect on the toymaker. The first few toys came out fine...

But the next batch looked stranger...

The toymaker began churning out hundreds of little Alfie dolls. Santa tried to turn it off, but it just kept going.

Santa glared angrily at Alfie. "The toymaker will take weeks to fix and there are still hundreds of toys to make."

"I'm s..s..sorry," sniffed Alfie.

"I'll have to give these dolls instead," said Santa sadly.

That year, instead of roller skates or a football, hundreds of children received Alfie dolls...

...and they were the most popular toy ever! Next year, Santa and his elves had requests for thousands more.

So the elves fixed the toymaker to make Alfie dolls and Santa put Alfie in charge – as long as he stayed on the outside this time.

Chapter 2

The fake Santa

It was the night before Christmas. Everyone in Firtown was fast asleep. Everyone except Santa, that is.

At every home, he parked his sleigh...

squeezed down the chimney...

filled the stockings with presents...

nibbled the
food left by
the children…

climbed back up
the chimney…

and raced on
to the house
next door.

Soon, Santa was ready to visit another town. But his reindeer were getting thirsty.

"I need a drink," said Rudolph. "Me too," gasped Prancer.

"Let's fly back to that river we passed," said Santa.

In no time, the reindeer were sipping ice cold river water.

Santa checked his watch. "Hurry up, boys," he said, nervously. "It'll soon be dawn."

They were about to take off, when an angry cry came from beyond the trees.

"Hey, you. Stop!"

A crowd of people stomped up to Santa. Some of them were still in their night clothes.

"How dare you upset my children!" yelled a woman. "You ought to be locked up!" shrieked another.

24

Santa was totally confused. "What are they talking about?" whispered Rudolph. "I've no idea," said Santa.

Suddenly a snowball hurtled from the crowd and hit Santa right on the nose.

"Ouch!" he cried. "What was that for?"

"Get him!" bellowed a man. All at once, snowball after snowball pelted Santa.

He jumped into his sleigh.

Let's get out of here!

Santa's reindeer carried him away to safety. "I can't understand it," he sniffed. "People usually like me."

"Something strange is going on here," said Dancer.

"Hey, look down there," Rudolph called excitedly. "A sleigh just like ours."

Santa peered over the side of his sleigh. A similar one was parked outside a house below. "Let's take a look," he said.

27

Close up, Santa saw that the sleigh was old and tattered. The 'reindeer' tied to it was really a horse with antlers strapped on.

Santa followed a trail of footprints inside. There in the living room stood... another Santa! Two small children sat tearfully by a Christmas tree.

"I made a mistake, kids," growled the other Santa. "You've been naughty, so I'm taking back all your presents."

Drop that sack, you thief!

"Rats!" snapped the man, seeing the real Santa. Grabbing his sack, the fake Santa rushed out.

The crook leapt into his sleigh full of stolen presents and raced away. Santa ran up to Rudolph. "Follow that sleigh!" he roared.

They stormed through the snow and soon caught up. The thief jumped off his sleigh and ran down a narrow alley.

At the end of the alley was a
wall. The tall crook sprang
over the top, but it was too
high for Santa.

I'll fix that faker.

Santa ran back to his sleigh.
He flew up over the wall and
hovered above the crook.
"Hey, you!" he cried.

As the crook looked up, Santa emptied the contents of his sack. The fake Santa was squashed by a shower of falling presents.

Santa took the thief back to the houses he'd robbed. At each one, the fake Santa gave back the stolen presents.

Hooray for the real Santa!

Then Santa made his last delivery in Firtown – to the local police.

Chapter 3

Santa's day off

Of all the days of the year,
Santa likes December 26th
best. It's his day off.

After one very tiring Christmas, Santa was looking forward to his day of rest.

He snuggled into his softest armchair, with a mug of hot chocolate and a slice of sticky Christmas cake.

As Santa settled down with a big book, two elves burst in.

"We can't get into our house," wailed Paddy.

"There's a huge polar bear blocking the way," added Pip.

Santa sighed and followed
the elves to their home.

A fierce polar bear was
pacing up and down outside.

"If I had some meat, I could
lure her away," said Santa.

"There are some sausages in
our kitchen," suggested Pip.
"If only we could get to them."

Santa had an idea. He crept around the back of the house. Then he climbed up to the chimney and squeezed inside.

Seconds later, he emerged carrying a furry white bundle.

"A polar bear cub!" cried Pip. "He must have climbed in through an open window."

"That's why the mother bear wouldn't let you in," said Santa. "She was protecting him."

The two animals happily plodded off across the snow.

Now I can get back to my cake.

Thank you, Santa.

Santa had just settled back in his armchair, when another worried elf rushed in.

"Calm down, Marco," Santa soothed. "What's the matter?"

"We accidentally left someone off this year's list," cried the elf.

"Get a bike from the store room," said Santa, wearily. "I'll get my sleigh ready."

An hour later, Santa landed at Jason's house.

As Santa carried the bike to the back door, he heard voices.

"Perhaps you'll get your red bike next year, son," said a man.

Oh. Okay, Dad.

Santa looked down at the bike. It was blue. He took a deep breath and returned to his sleigh.

One trip to the North Pole
later, Santa was back – with a
red bike. Jason was overjoyed.
Santa headed north again.

He was almost home, when
he heard a cry from below.
"Help! Someone help me!"
Santa went to investigate.

A farmer was standing by a frozen lake.

"My sheep have wandered onto the ice, Santa," he said. "And it's starting to crack."

Please don't let them drown.

Santa flew his sleigh just above the sheep. "Hover here, boys!" he cried to his reindeer.

Santa gently eased himself over the edge of his sleigh. Reaching down, he grabbed a sheep and lifted it to safety.

Baa!

Baa!

One by one, he bundled the sheep into his sleigh. The ice finally cracked open just as the last animal left the ice.

44

Santa returned the sheep to the grateful farmer.

Santa was exhausted. He returned to his sleigh and set a course for the North Pole.

When he got home, he staggered into his living room.

"My hot chocolate will be cold by now," sighed Santa. "And I bet that cake is as dry as dust."
But he was in for a surprise.

On the table by his armchair stood a mug of steaming hot chocolate, a pile of fresh cream cakes and a stack of storybooks.

Even Santa's slippers were warming by the newly lit fire. Elves flooded into the room.

"How kind," smiled Santa.
"Our pleasure, Santa," said Paddy. "You've shown us that kindness is what Christmas is all about."

Series editor: Lesley Sims

First published in 2006 by Usborne Publishing Ltd., Usborne House,
83-85 Saffron Hill, London EC1N 8RT, England. www.usborne.com
Copyright © 2006 Usborne Publishing Ltd.

48